To Ruth and Smiler, with love

First published in Great Britain in 1998 by Ragged Bears Limited,
Ragged Appleshaw, Andover, Hampshire SP11 9HX
Copyright © 1998 David Ellwand
The right of David Ellwand to be identified as the author and
illustrator of this work has been asserted
ALL RIGHTS RESERVED
Layouts by Janet McCallum
A CIP record of this book is available from the British Library
ISBN 1 85714 1466
Printed in Hong Kong

ALFRED'S CAMERA

A collection of Picture Puzzles
by David Ellwand

Ragged Bears

Alfred is well-known for miles around,
he's the finest photographer in the town
but in his house there's so much mess
and things get lost, to his distress.

You see the naughty, muddily, Pointer pup
has yet to learn he must tidy up,
he needs to learn if he puts them away,
he'll find things again the very next day.

Today Alfred is in a terrible stew.
He has an important job that he's got to do.
His best friend Sport is coming for tea,
it's his birthday and Alfred's present will be...

to take a picture of Sport for all to see...
but Alfred... can't find his CAMERA!

So turn the page and see if you
can find the camera before they do.

'Where's my camera?' Alfred said as thoughtfully he scratched

but other things are hiding around me? A horseshoe,

my shell, whistles, a spoon. I'd better tidy all these soon.'

to the place where all the other shells lay.

a starfish, a boat and a boot.

But WHERE IS MY CAMERA?'

In amongst the cars

and trucks Alfred found three rubber ducks.

But he still couldn't find his camera.

All the bears were pleased to see that they were invited to Sport's birthday tea.

Is that a jug on Teddy's head?

'Was that the doorbell?' Alfred cried. 'Oh good,

it's you Sport, come inside!

I need to find my camera instead.'

'WHERE'S MY CAMERA?'

said Sport,

the fruit bowl and threw it all out.

'You're the messiest dog ever known!'

Alfred was starting to feel rather sick, from his

and cried 'But where's my camera,

He dug through and found his collar,

toys and a brush

we're in such a rush?'

and on to the floor, fell tumbling his glasses

He opened the cupboard

'Please pick those up Sport

and brushes galore. His dog bowl, some flowers,

a teapot too,

and bring them with you.'

If we don't find it soon, there will be no time for tea.

Sport sighed, 'WHERE IS YOUR CAMERA to take a picture of me?

but it feels as though we've

Look here's a cup, a moth and a fork. I really think

we need to talk. It was kind of you to buy me these flowers

been searching for hours.'

And underneath the cotton reels, the balls of wool

'Cheer up, Sport, don't pull a face, I think I know of one more place.'

a red bus and ....

and knitting needles, in his sewing box Alfred found

a tin of dog food, big and round,

THE CAMERA!

'Come on Sport and pose for me,

then we can have your birthday tea!'

Alfred's search is now at an end,
and he can enjoy the day with his friend.
But if he'd looked harder he might have found
many <u>more</u> objects lying around.

Did you find everything Alfred saw?
If you did, you could now find a few more.
So turn back the pages and take a look
at all the other objects hidden in this book!

P.S. Alfred has also lost his mouse and his lead. Did you find them?